Blue whale

Tiger shark

Killer whale

wilkes

The Golden Book of
Sharks and Whales

By Kathleen N. Daly
Illustrated by James Spence

Captain Mark Merdinyan, Consultant

A GOLDEN BOOK • NEW YORK
Western Publishing Company, Inc., Racine, Wisconsin 53404

Hammerhead shark

Mako shark

Pteranodon

Tyrannosaurus rex

Plesiosaur

The planet on which we live is called Earth, but it is mostly covered with water—the oceans and seas of the world.

Life began in those waters long, long ago, and today the seas are still teeming with billions of creatures. Among them are the whales and sharks, which have been there for millions of years.

Sharks lived in the oceans long before there were whales, and even before there were dinosaurs or any other animals on land.

Bluefin tuna

Bull shark

Amazing Facts About Sharks

Sharks are fish, but what amazing fish they are!

A shark doesn't have a bone in its body. Its skeleton is made of cartilage, or gristle—tough material like that of your ears. All other fish have skeletons of bone, and so they are called bony fish.

The skin of a bony fish is covered with smooth scales. A shark's skin is covered with small razor-sharp teeth called denticles. These can cause scratches and deep cuts if rubbed.

8

Black-tipped shark

Mako shark

Denticles are similar to the teeth in your mouth. They have a soft inner pulp covered with dentin and hard enamel.

The massive tooth-filled jaws of a shark are usually found on the underside of its head. It can open its jaws very wide and move them forward to grasp prey.

A shark has row upon row of sharp teeth. If a tooth falls out, another one moves forward to replace it. Sometimes the new tooth, which is larger than the old one, is in place within a day. The shark may go through a thousand sets of teeth in a lifetime.

A Shark's Senses

A shark has extraordinary senses. Sometimes the shark is called a "swimming nose," for it has a remarkable sense of smell. It can easily detect prey in the dark or buried in the sand.

A shark also has a remarkable sensitivity to vibrations in the water around it. It can feel the movements made by other animals hundreds of feet away.

Sharks can hear sounds from thousands of feet away and can tell the direction from which a sound is coming.

Mako shark

Billfish

Gill slits

How Sharks Breathe

A fish breathes by taking in water through its mouth and passing the water over its gills. As the water meets the blood vessels in the gills, it releases oxygen, which then passes into the fish's bloodstream. In people and other mammals the lungs do the same job as gills.

Most fish have one gill on each side of their head, covered with a flap of skin. As the cover opens and closes, water keeps moving over the gills.

A shark has five to seven gills on each side of its head and no covering flap, so a shark must keep moving to keep the water flowing over its gills. However, divers recently reported seeing nurse sharks resting sleepily in underwater caves and not moving at all! Perhaps the sharks were taking advantage of oxygen-rich fresh water seeping into the caves. No one knows for sure.

Different Kinds of Sharks

Sharks are not only different from other kinds of fish, they are different from each other. There are at least 350 different kinds of sharks that we know about right now. Another new kind may be discovered at any moment.

The hammerhead shark is a graceful, powerful swimmer. No one knows why it has such a strangely shaped head. But it can zero in on its prey with the help of sensitive nostrils and eyes on either side of its hammer-shaped head.

The tiger shark has a huge blunt, rounded nose. This shark is striped like a tiger, and it is as fierce as a tiger when hunting. It is one of the most powerful sharks and often goes after huge marine turtles.

Hammerhead shark

Sea turtle

Tiger shark

The blue shark is sleek and slender. Everything about it is long: its body, its snout, its tail, and its fins. Its color is a beautiful deep-sea blue, shading to white underneath. The blue shark swims very fast and can easily catch speedy flying fish.

The large mako shark is lively, athletic, and dangerous. It has been known to leap 20 feet into the air. If the mako lands in a fisherman's boat, it can cause a lot of damage to the boat and its passengers.

Porbeagles grow to about 12 feet in length. We don't usually think of sharks as being playful, but porbeagles have been seen playing with timber and other floating objects at the surface of the water.

The thresher has a tail longer than its body. The whole fish may grow to about 20 feet. Nobody knows for sure how the thresher uses its long tail. Some people think its tail is used like a whip to stun and scare whole schools of small fish.

Thresher shark

Blue shark

13

Fur seal

The Great White Shark

Of all the fantastic creatures of the ocean, the great white shark is the most feared. It is sometimes known as "the man-eater," for it has attacked people in the water. But mostly it feeds on large fish and sea mammals, such as seals and otters.

The great white can measure up to 25 feet long and weigh as much as 4,500 pounds.

It is truly a magnificent creature, with a splendidly powerful body, huge jaws, and extraordinary senses, perfectly designed for hunting and catching its prey. Books have been written about the great white, many stories have been told, and movies have been made, but not very much is known about this huge creature. Like other animals of the deep, the great white is a mystery to us and difficult to study, for it is hard to find in the ocean.

With the help of modern diving gear, people can now explore the underwater world. But sea animals are still hard to find because they may not appear at the right time, or they may take off more rapidly than people can follow.

Another reason that large sharks cannot be studied is that they seldom live more than a few days in captivity. They need the vastness of the oceans to survive. The sharks that you see in aquariums are the smaller ones, such as the lemon and the nurse sharks.

Great white shark
hunting seal

A Nurse Shark and a Carpet Shark

Not all sharks look and act like speedy torpedoes. Nurse sharks spend much of their lives lying on the sea floor or drifting among corals in a reef. They are so sluggish that bathers have stepped on them and have been bitten by the sharks, which don't like to be disturbed.

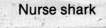

Nurse shark

Moray eel

Butterfly fish

The nurse shark is the shark most often seen in an aquarium. It can be from 10 to 14 feet in length and weigh up to 350 pounds.

The wobbegong, or carpet shark, is also a bottom dweller and is even lazier than the nurse shark. Its body is flattened and it really does look like a carpet. The wobbegong has blotches, stripes, and rings on its body, with a fringe and tassels around the edges. Even though they may be brightly colored, wobbegongs are difficult to see as they lie quietly on rocks, weeds, and corals, waiting for a fish or a shrimp to drop in for dinner.

Carpet shark

The Biggest Fish of All

The whale shark is the biggest fish in the sea. It is between 35 and 50 feet long and weighs about 13 tons. And yet this huge creature hardly ever eats anything bigger than a shrimp.

The whale shark's mouth is at the front of its head rather than on the underside. It cruises around with its mouth open to let in plankton, a kind of sea soup filled with tiny plants and animals. At the entrance to the whale shark's throat are the gill rakers, which are very fine threads that form a kind of net to strain food from the water.

The whale shark's skin has a marvelous checkerboard pattern, unlike anything else in nature.

We are used to thinking of sharks as being fiercely aggressive, but sharks are full of surprises. Many divers have hitched rides on the backs of the enormous, peaceful creatures known as whale sharks.

Whale sharks and divers

Megafish

The second largest fish in the sea is also a shark—the basking shark. It can be from 27 to 30 feet long. Like the whale shark, it is a slow-moving plankton eater.

It looks more "sharky" than the whale shark, with dark skin, a pointed snout, and small eyes. It swims with its mouth wide open to catch plankton, which it sifts through long, slender gill rakers.

Sometimes these huge creatures leap high in the air. Nobody knows why, but perhaps it is to rid the body of pesky sea lice. Perhaps it is to say hello to other basking sharks in the neighborhood.

Basking sharks

An exciting new discovery in the world of sharks was hauled onto a U.S. Navy ship in 1976, tangled up in an anchor. Nothing like it had ever been seen before. This shark was 14½ feet long, weighed 1,653 pounds, and was a plankton eater. Its cavelike mouth glowed with silvery light. Scientists think that the glow might have attracted shrimps and small fish. It was nicknamed "Megamouth" (big mouth).

It is amazing to think that such a large fish could remain undiscovered until now. Who knows how many more kinds of fish are hidden in the deep?

Megamouth

Eggs and Babies

Unlike other fish, most sharks give birth to live young, not eggs. Most sharks have six to twelve young at a time, but some, like the hammerhead and tiger sharks, give birth to as many as forty babies at a time.

A baby shark is born with a strong swimming body and a mouthful of sharp teeth. It is ready to hunt and kill from the instant it is born.

A few sharks produce tough, leathery egg capsules that attach themselves to corals, rocks, and seaweed. Inside the rubbery purse the baby shark grows like a bird within its egg. Empty egg cases of sharks often wash up on the beach. They are sometimes called mermaid's purses.

Some baby sharks are born with a yolk attached to their body—a built-in feed bag. They feed on the rich yolk as they grow.

Dusky shark

Mermaid's purses

Skates and Rays

Skates and rays are related to sharks. They, too, have bodies made of cartilage, but their bodies are flattened out, with side fins that look like enormous wings.

The manta ray has a "wing" spread of about 20 feet and is sometimes called the devilfish, but it never attacks people. It flaps peacefully through the water like a very large butterfly.

A stingray can be as small as a dinner plate or as large as a bathtub. It has a long, whiplike tail with poisonous barbs.

When in danger, electric rays send out powerful electric shocks that can stun or kill their enemies.

Rays give birth to live young, but skates produce rubbery eggs like those of some sharks. Their flat bodies look like underwater kites. Skates often live in shallow water and can be seen lying on the bottom.

Manta ray

Electric ray

Skate

Humpback whales

About Whales

Whales are the biggest creatures that have ever lived on Earth. They live in the ocean, but unlike sharks, whales are not fish. They are mammals, like people, elephants, seals, dogs, and cats. There are about eighty different kinds of whales.

A mammal is an animal that has lungs and breathes air. It gives birth to live young, not eggs. It also has hair on its body. The young feed on their mother's milk.

When a baby whale calf is born, tail first, its mother quickly pushes it up to the surface for its first breath of air. Then the baby has its first meal.

Whales are sociable creatures and like each other's company. They travel together in groups called pods. All the grown-ups help to take care of the babies, and the youngsters play together in a friendly and affectionate way.

Echolocation

Whales have an amazing way of "seeing" underwater. They send out sharp clicking sounds that travel rapidly through the water. When the sound waves hit an object, such as a fish, they bounce off and travel back to the whale. The whale can then figure out the size and shape of the object and how far away it is.

This method of "seeing" is called echolocation, or sonar. Submarines use sonar to find their way underwater. Bats use it to find their way at night.

As well as sonar clicking, whales make all kinds of other sounds: they groan, creak like rusty gates, squeal, moo like cows, and whistle and chirp like birds.

Nobody knows how whales make the sounds. They don't have vocal cords. Perhaps they can shift air around inside their bodies.

Right whale

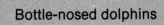
Bottle-nosed dolphins

Bowhead whale

Two Groups of Whales

Whales are divided into two groups: baleen whales and toothed whales.

Baleens are also called "the great whales" because of their enormous size. Yet as big as these creatures are, they feed only on the tiniest creatures of the sea, found in plankton. Plankton is made up of billions of tiny plants and animals that float in the water, drifting with the waves and tides. Plankton is an important food for many larger creatures. The baleens cruise with their huge mouths open and take in water and plankton. The food is then sifted through hairy fringes called baleen, or whalebone.

The Gray Whale

The California gray is a baleen whale well known to whale watchers. Every year it travels from icy waters to warm seas where its young are born.

After the young have learned to swim strongly, the whales return to the polar waters. The adults make a round trip of over 16,000 miles.

The gray whales are so regular in their habits that people know exactly where and when they will appear, and they come to watch the beautiful, peaceful creatures and to wish them well on their long journey.

Gray whale

The Blue Whale

The largest whale of all is the blue whale, which is bigger than the biggest dinosaur ever was. The blue whale can be over 100 feet long and can weigh 150 tons. That is more than 30 elephants or 2,000 people! Its heart weighs 1,200 pounds. Its tongue weighs one third of a ton and is as long as a small car.

And yet the blue whale eats only the tiniest creatures in the ocean. It filters krill, a tiny kind of shrimp, into its throat through its baleen sieve.

The infant blue whale is the biggest baby in the world. It may be as long as 25 feet at birth and weigh about 2 tons. Its mother's milk is very rich. The baby feeds about fifty times a day, drinking two and a half gallons at a time. It grows very fast.

Blue whale and calf

Sperm whale and giant squid

The Sperm Whale

The sperm whale is the largest of the toothed whales. It may be 60 feet long and weigh up to 60 tons. Females are smaller than males.

The sperm whale has teeth only in its lower jaw. It uses them to seize prey, not to chew it. The sperm whale swallows its prey whole. When its jaws are closed, its teeth fit neatly into sockets in its upper jaw.

The sperm whale has the thickest skin, called blubber, of any animal. In places the blubber is about 12 inches thick. And the sperm whale has the biggest brain of any animal. Its brain weighs 20 pounds.

This whale can dive down to a depth of more than 3,500 feet and stay underwater longer than an hour. In the darkness of the deep the sperm whale and the giant squid have mighty battles, for squid is this whale's favorite food. The whales often have numerous scars on their bodies made by the squid's whiplike tentacles and its arms, which are covered with suckerlike disks.

When the whale comes back to the surface, it breathes out the used-up air in a 20-foot-tall spout that comes from the nostril, which is called a blowhole.

The sperm whale is easy to identify because of its huge blunt-ended head, large tail flukes, and small flippers.

Sperm whale spouting through blowhole

The Orca, or Killer Whale

The orca gets its "killer" name from the fact that it is a mighty hunter. It travels in packs and may attack and kill other whales, including the mighty blue whale. It also eats seals, sea otters, and large fish, even the great white shark.

To catch a seal on an ice floe, the killer whale may jump up onto the ice, or it may dive underneath the ice and tip it so that the seal slides off into the water.

The killer whale has never been known to attack a human being. In fact, these beautiful black-and-white creatures have become star performers at oceanariums all over the world and are friendly and affectionate toward their trainers. The huge 6,000-pound animal will shoot out of the water at a trainer's command and plant a "kiss" on her cheek.

Orca hunting seal

This amazing behavior is possible because trainers ask this intelligent animal to perform actions that are quite close to their natural behavior. For example, in the wild, orca the hunter is always on the lookout for prey. Always curious, the whale hops above the water and leaps out of it to see what is going on. In captivity, the whale is still curious. It will leap up to look at a rope that the trainer holds higher and higher above the pool.

In the wild, these whales love each other's company. They are playful and affectionate with each other. So it's only natural for a whale to become fond of the trainers that feed it, play with it, and stroke it every day.

Orca "kissing" trainer

Harbor porpoise

Bottle-nosed dolphins

Dolphins and Porpoises

Dolphins and porpoises are small whales that are closely related to each other. Like their cousins the orcas, these whales are beautiful, playful, intelligent, and friendly.

Like all whales, dolphins and porpoises take good care of their young and of each other. They travel in large groups, and talk to each other by making clicking and chirping sounds. If one of the group is wounded, the others will gather around to help keep it afloat and breathing.

Ever since people have been to sea in ships, sailors have noticed that dolphins and porpoises love to ride the waves made by the bow of a ship.

Captive dolphins and porpoises learn to perform in the same way as killer whales and seem to enjoy the company of their trainers.

The Beluga, or White, Whale

Another whale that seems exceptionally friendly to people is the beluga. It usually lives in the icy waters near the North Pole, where its pale color blends in with the ice and snow of the land. It grows to be about 18 feet long.

Belugas like company and travel together in large packs. They talk to one another so much that they have been nicknamed "sea canaries."

Once in a while a beluga swims away from its friends and travels into inland waters, where it makes friends with people in small boats and rubber rafts. It will stay a while and then mysteriously disappear.

Beluga whales

Humpback whale and calf

The Humpback Whale

The humpback, a baleen whale, is famous for its songs.

Like most whales, the humpbacks travel together in groups called pods. Whales keep an eye on each other by "spy hopping"—leaping up out of the water—and by sending out sound signals.

The humpback whale sometimes makes sounds that seem to us like mysterious and wonderful songs It seems that each year the same group of humpbacks will sing a new song, adding to the old one and leaving out some of last year's notes.

The recorded songs of the humpback whale have been sent into outer space, along with other Earth sounds, on the spaceships *Voyager I* and *II*. The songs may someday be heard by beings in another galaxy.

Humpback whales making
bubble net to trap fish

Intelligence

Whales may have the biggest brains of any creatures on Earth,
but that doesn't necessarily mean they are the smartest animals.

Whales—or at least the dolphins and orcas that we have come to
know through aquariums and movies—have a wonderful ability to
learn and to imitate. They also make up games of their own. Most
whales seem to be able to talk to each other, and the humpbacks sing
songs that change and grow from year to year.

Whales do many things that seem to depend on thinking. For
example, humpbacks work together to make a bubble net underwater
to trap schools of fish. But are these creatures really thinking, or are
they just acting on instinct? Nobody knows the answer to this
question.

And what about sharks? Are they stupid because they have small brains for their size? Definitely not! They are smart enough to have been around for 300 million years. Their brains are perfect for doing shark things.

Whales have perfect brains for whales. Sharks have perfect brains for sharks. And people have perfect brains for people. It's interesting to compare the different things that each kind of animal can and cannot do.

Mako shark

Dolphin fish

Octopus

Whales and sharks are only two kinds of the many billions of creatures that live in the oceans. We know very little about them, for it is difficult to study the creatures of the deep. But we do know that we must protect these mysterious and marvelous animals and the waters in which they live.

There have been times when whales have been trapped by ice or stranded on beaches. Suddenly people of many nations get together to help the whales. People do care about the creatures of the sea. For, after all, it's up to us to make sure that they will be around for millions of years to come.

Index

Sperm whale

Beluga whale

Great white shark

Hammerhead shark

Blue shark